D0045765

A Beginning-to-Read Book

What's in the Woods, Dear Dragon?

by Margaret Hillert
Illustrated by David Schimmell

NORWOOD HOUSE PRESS

DEAR CAREGIVER,

The *Beginning-to-Read* series is a carefully written collection of classic readers you may remember from your own childhood. Each book features text comprised of common sight words to provide your child ample practice reading the words that appear most frequently in written text. The many additional details in the pictures enhance the story and offer the opportunity for you to help your child expand oral language and develop comprehension.

Begin by reading the story to your child, followed by letting him or her read familiar words and soon your child will be able to read the story independently. At each step of the way, be sure to praise your reader's efforts to build his or her confidence as an independent reader. Discuss the pictures and encourage your child to make connections between the story and his or her own life. At the end of the story, you will find reading activities and a word list that will help your child practice and strengthen beginning reading skills.

Above all, the most important part of the reading experience is to have fun and enjoy it!

Shannon Cannon

Shannon Cannon,
Literacy Consultant

Norwood House Press • P.O. Box 316598 • Chicago, Illinois 60631
For more information about Norwood House Press please visit our website at *www.norwoodhousepress.com* or call 866-565-2900.

Text copyright ©2014 by Margaret Hillert. Illustrations and cover design copyright ©2014 by Norwood House Press, Inc. All rights reserved. No part of this book may be reproduced or utilized in any form or by any means without written permission from the publisher.

LIBRARY OF CONGRESS CATALOGING-IN-PUBLICATION DATA
Hillert, Margaret.
    What's in the woods, dear dragon? / by Margaret Hillert ; illustrated by David Schimmell.
        pages cm. -- (A beginning-to-read book)
    Summary: "A boy and his pet dragon go for an adventure in the woods. They
learn about trees, animals, and fun activities that can take place along the
way. This title includes reading activities and a word list"-- Provided by publisher.
    ISBN 978-1-59953-606-4 (library edition : alk. paper)
    ISBN 978-1-60357-600-0 (ebook)
[1. Dragons--Fiction. 2. Nature--Fiction.] I. Schimmell, David,
illustrator. II. Title. III. Title: What is in the woods, dear dragon?
PZ7.H558Wgm 2013
[E]--dc23

                                                2013010627

Manufactured in the United States of America in Stevens Point, Wisconsin.
243R—092013

It's a good day for a walk.
Do you want to come with me?

Oh, yes Father.
I like to walk and see things.

Dragon, Dragon, Dragon.
You cannot sit all day.
It is not good for you.

Come on. Come on.
Get up.
Come with us.

We will go to the woods.
A lot of trees make a woods.

Look what I can do.
Can you see this rabbit?
Maybe we will see some rabbits.

Look what I can do with this.
This is fun to do.

What a good day it is.
Here we are in the woods.

The trees are so pretty.
It makes me happy.

Some trees are big.

Some trees are little.

Look up there.
It is pretty, too.

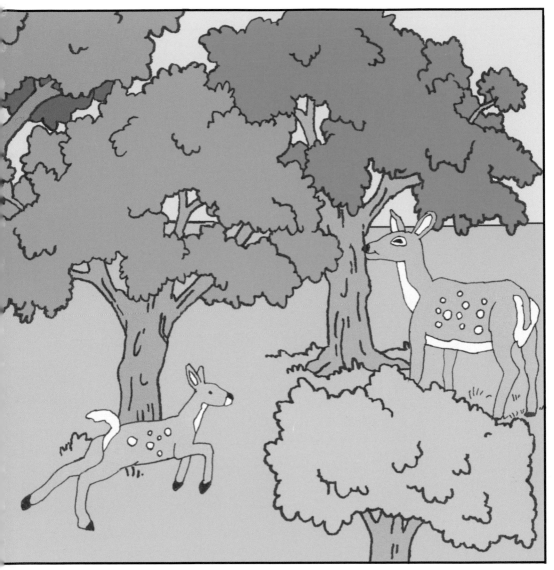

It is a baby deer.
It runs away.
It wants to go to the mother deer.

And look up there.
Something is in there.

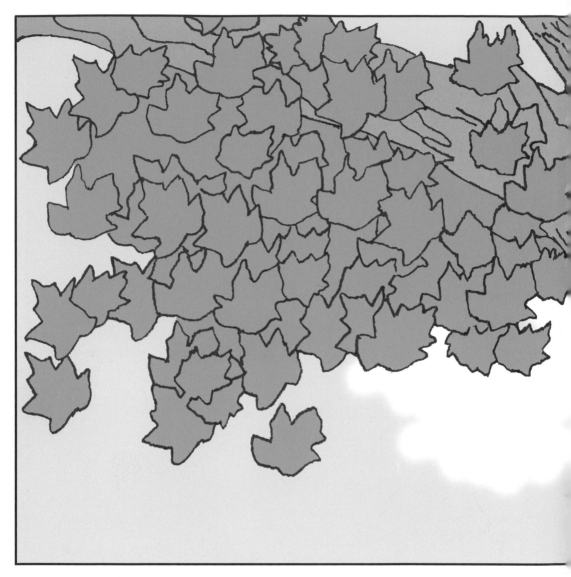

Oh, oh see what it is?
A big squirrel.
It likes this spot.

It likes the trees.

Birds like the trees, too.
They make homes here.
They lay eggs here.
Baby birds come out of the eggs.

Look at the eggs.
Some babies are out.

They are pretty.
They will get big and fly away.

We cannot fly.

But we can run!
Run, run, run!

We will run home.
We will run to Mother.

Mother, Mother.
Here we are.

Father is coming too!

Here I am with you, Dear Dragon
and here you are with me.

What a good, good day to
walk in the woods with Father.

READING REINFORCEMENT

The following activities support the findings of the National Reading Panel that determined the most effective components for reading instruction are: Phonemic Awareness, Phonics, Vocabulary, Fluency, and Text Comprehension.

Phonemic Awareness: The /w/ sound

Oral Blending: Say the beginning sounds listed below and ask your child to say the word formed by adding the /**w**/ sound to the end:

/w/ + ill = will	/w/ + ing = wing	/w/ + all = wall
/w/ + eek = week	/w/ + ith = with	/w/ + ell = well
/w/ + ood = wood	/w/ + alk - walk	/w/ + in = win
/w/ + ash = wash	/w/ + ide = wide	/w/ + ink = wink

Phonics: The letter Ww

1. Demonstrate how to form the letters **W** and **w** for your child.

2. Have your child practice writing **W** and **w** at least three times each.

3. Ask your child to point to the words in the book that begin with the letter **w**.

4. Write down the following words and ask your child to circle the letter **w** in each word:

how	walk	wait	we	flower
who	what	woods	when	with
now	work	away	fewer	went

Vocabulary: Suffix –ful

1. Explain to your child that the suffix –ful means "full of".

2. Say the following words and ask your child to add the suffix –ful to each one:

   joy + ful = joyful   care + ful = careful   thank + ful = thankful

   help + ful = helpful   grate + ful = grateful   truth + ful = truthful

   respect + ful = respectful   thought + ful = thoughtful

   peace + ful = peaceful

3. Write each word on a separate piece of paper.

4. Read each word aloud for your child.

5. Take turns with your child pointing to a word and describing a time when you were...(...joyful, careful, thankful, etc.)

Fluency: Shared Reading

1. Reread the story to your child at least two more times while your child tracks the print by running a finger under the words as they are read. Ask your child to read the words he or she knows with you.

2. Reread the story taking turns, alternating readers between sentences or pages.

Text Comprehension: Discussion Time

1. Ask your child to retell the sequence of events in the story.

2. To check comprehension, ask your child the following questions:

   - We cannot fly, but on page 22 what animal can fly?
   - What things do they see in the woods?
   - Where do you like to go on a walk? Why?
   - What is your favorite animal? Why?

WORD LIST

What's in the Woods, Dear Dragon? uses the 80 words listed below.

The **8** words bolded below serve as an introduction to new vocabulary, while the other 72 are pre-primer. You may wish to write the words on index cards and use them to help your child build automatic word recognition. Regular practice with these words will enhance your child's fluency in reading connected text.

a	day	I	on	to
all	dear	in	out	too
am	**deer**	is		**trees**
and	do	it	pretty	
are	dragon	it's		up
at			**rabbit(s)**	us
away	**eggs**	lay	run(s)	
		like(s)		walk
babies	Father	little	see	want(s)
baby	fly	look	sit	we
big	for	lot	so	what
birds	fun		some	will
but		make(s)	something	with
	get	maybe	spot	**woods**
can	go	me	**squirrel**	
cannot	good	Mother		you
come			the	yes
coming	happy	not	there	
	here		they	
	home(s)	of	things	
		oh	this	

ABOUT THE AUTHOR Margaret Hillert has written over 80 books for children who are just learning to read. Her books have been translated into many different languages and over a million children throughout the world have read her books. She first started writing poetry as a child and has continued to write for children and adults throughout her life. A first grade teacher for 34 years, Margaret is now retired from teaching and lives in Michigan where she likes to write, take walks in the morning, and care for her three cats.

Photograph by Glenna Washburn

ABOUT THE ILLUSTRATOR David Schimmell served as a professional firefighter for 23 years before hanging up his boots and helmet to devote himself to working as an illustrator of children's books. David has happily created illustrations for the New Dear Dragon books as well as other artwork for educational and retail book projects. Born and raised in Evansville, Indiana, he lives there today with his wife and family.